God bles!
Jesus Loves you!

Many people today are taught that dinosaurs died off millions of years ago. But according to the Bible and real scientific evidence, that is simply not true. Did you know that dinosaur bones have been found with blood vessels in them? That's great evidence that dinosaur bones can't be that old. Furthermore, this book is based on sightings of a dinosaur by people who live in the jungles of Africa today. They call him "Mokele Mbembe". Good luck pronouncing that!

Did you know that the Bible also talks about dinosaurs and that they lived alongside people? It's true! God made dinosaurs and Adam and Eve on day six of creation week. Not only that, but God told Noah to put two of every creature on the ark, including dinosaurs! They lived through the flood, and it appears a few may still be lurking around the jungles today. That's why we have so many stories passed down through the centuries of dragons, which are really dinosaurs, and why we still hear about sightings today. Cool, huh?

This book is about a young girl and her father on an adventure of a lifetime. It's also a story of forgiveness, trust, and faith in a loving God. May you come to know him and his joy.

Have fun!

MOKEE

A Dinosaur Adventure

Written by Steve & Carrie Levinson
Illustration by Bill Looney

For more information about the author go to

www.genesisseminars.org

Here you can find information about how to book a creation seminar at your church!

Also, listen to your local Christian radio station for "Creation Discoveries", a one-minute nugget of truth about how God made things so awesome.

Acknowledgement

I want to thank the Lord Jesus Christ for this project because he is the one who helped me and Carrie create it.

Carrie and I will never forget putting a canoe in our living room, complete with tree branches and a "river" to get us in the right mood to begin writing.

And I want to thank my wife, Karen, and daughter, Emily, for editing the project.

Preface

This book is based on many sightings of a dinosaur that has been seen near the border countries of Cameroon and Congo, Africa. There is an area of thick rainforest about the size of Florida that is practically unexplored by scientists. Locals living in the region have seen a large dinosaur-like animal with a long neck and long tail coming up out of the Congo River for years. They call it Mokele Mbembe, which means "the one who stops the flow of rivers". The dinosaur fits the description of the creature described in the book of Job, chapter 40. This, along with other sightings around the world, is convincing evidence that some dinosaurs could very well still be alive today.

Chapters

A Lifetime Adventure

Chapter 1

Gone Fishing

"Can you hand me the torch, Papa?" I asked.

It was a very dark night, and Papa and I were getting ready to go on our weekly fishing trip. Summer was the best time of the year for a certain type of fish we were after, the speckled Goliath Tiger Fish. One adult fish could easily weigh up to one-hundred pounds and could feed our whole village of ten families.

"Sure, honey, here you go, and be careful not to get any of the hakonish on you or you will stink for a week!" Papa said.

"Okay, I won't," I said.

Hakonish was a kind of black gooey tar that was flammable and great for making torches. There was only one place that we knew of to find it: the flaming pools of Walanimka. Not only was this stuff sticky, but it was stinky, and the smoke from it was great for keeping the mosquitos away. In this part of the world, mosquitos carried many deadly diseases, so hakonish was really necessary.

"I think we are just about packed and ready to shove off, Zualoo. Put the torch in the front of the boat and go get Poppy while I finish cutting up the bait," Papa said.

Poppy was our African hound dog that loved to go on our fishing trips. She was welcome because she was good protection for us. She had scared off many wildcats and saved our lives on more than one occasion.

"Come here, girl! Jump in the boat! Good girl. Okay, Papa, are we ready to go?" I asked.

"Actually, I believe we are. Now untie the rope and give us a good shove off," Papa said.

As we began our journey into the blackness of the night, the temperature must have still been around 95 degrees, and we were drenched in sweat. If the smell of the torches didn't keep the mosquitos away, our body odor sure would.

"I love fishing with you," I said as we set out. "Will you tell me some stories about Jesus' disciples, like which ones were fishermen and why he chose some smelly men to be his closest friends?"

"Well, let's see. There were four of them: Simon, who Jesus later called Peter; Andrew, his brother; and James and John who were also brothers. As far as why the Lord chose them, I don't know. Perhaps because he wanted to show us that he can use just plain folks like you and me to do his work. He can even use little girls! Did you know that there was a little girl in the Old Testament that God used to help a leper be healed?" Papa asked.

"No! Could you tell me that story instead? Was she my age?" I wondered.

"Well, the Bible doesn't say, but I kinda think she was probably a young girl just like you. Let's see... There was this man named Naaman who was like a top general in the Syrian army. His name actually means 'beautiful', but what's strange is that he had a disease called leprosy that deforms the body. During a war with Israel, Syria had captured this little girl," Papa explained.

"What was her name?" I interrupted.

"Again, the Bible doesn't say, but it's not important. And that's the point. You see, sometimes God wants to use people who are just plain everyday folks or who aren't famous with big names. There are many stories like this in the Bible. Now, where was I? Oh. So this little girl became a slave, and guess who she just happened to work for?"

"Uhhh, Naaman?" I guessed.

"That's right. Very good. One day the little girl suggested that Naaman meet a prophet named Elisha who could ask God to heal him."

Papa interrupted his story and directed me. "Paddle a little to your right, away from the branches."

He continued, "So Naaman went to see him, but when Elisha told him to dip seven times in the Jordan River, he refused because the water was muddy."

"But why did Elisha tell him to dip seven times in a muddy river? Sounds strange," I commented.

"Yeah, it does sound weird, but what matters to God is that we obey him even in the times we don't understand."

"Sorry, Papa. I don't mean to keep interrupting you," I said apologetically.

"You ask all the questions you want. That's how you learn. You know, there's actually a lot of symbolism in this story," Papa continued.

"Symbolism?" I asked.

"That means the characters and events in the story may relate to something in life to teach us a lesson. Like Naaman, for instance. He had leprosy, and if you had this disease, it was incurable by man. It represents the sinner who is unclean, and there is nothing you can do to make yourself clean before God. In other words, only God can forgive you of your sins, not man," Papa explained.

"Oh, wow. That's a pretty neat way to think about it," I said.

"Mm-hmm. You see, Naaman was a man of great military honor and power, but he was also prideful and thought some other clean river was better to wash in," Papa said.

"Boy, he sure wouldn't want to bathe in this murky river, would he?" I giggled.

"Probably not, especially since there are piranhas in it," Papa smiled, making his hands into chomping fish jaws.

"So what did he do?" I wondered.

"Well, at first Naaman refused to listen to the little girl's advice to go to Elisha, so instead he went to the king of Israel with a lot of money thinking he could buy a cure. So what do you think this may mean?" Papa quizzed.

"Hmm. Well, ahh, I don't know," I said as I thought about it.

"Can you buy your way to heaven?" Papa prompted.

"No," I said.

"How about by being a good person?" he continued.

"No – oh, now I get it! Some people think that God will forgive them or wash them of their sins because of what they do," I said.

"That's right. They think that they can come to God their way, but Jesus said, 'I am the way, the truth and the life, and no one comes to the Father except through me.'

Finally, Naaman followed Elisha's request, and after dipping in the river for the seventh time, he was made clean. The Bible says his skin became like a child's skin. He had a baby face again. Isn't that great of God to not only restore his health but to also give him a youthful look again?" Papa asked, smiling.

"Yeah, that is awesome. So did Naaman give the girl her freedom from being his slave? Did he thank her?" I asked.

"Once again, the Bible doesn't say, but he did come to know that God is the only God and decide that he wouldn't worship false idols anymore. So you see how one little girl influenced a man of great power and authority? Even though she was a slave of Naaman, she didn't think of herself. She realized that he did not know the true God and thought if he'd only go see Elisha that he would not only get healed on the outside but his heart would get cleaned on the inside too. And that's just what happened," Papa concluded.

"Wow, I hope I can be like that girl, Papa," I said.

"Well, honey, you just be what God wants you to be. You'll figure that out if you just obey his word and listen to his voice. It's not important to be what other people are like. What is important is what God wants you to be like. You are unique, so be unique for God," Papa said as he clutched my hand.

Chapter 2

I'm Hooked

"The current is really strong tonight, Papa. I hardly have to paddle at all," I commented.

"That's great, but keep the boat in the center of the river," Papa said.

The Congo River was as black as the night, and because there were low clouds and no moonlight, it was especially hard to see anything past 30 feet. While I tried to keep the boat steady and straight, Papa was busy baiting the hooks.

"You're doing a great job, Zualoo," Papa said.

"Thanks, Papa, and you're doing a great job, too. I've never seen anyone do that better than you," I said, and Papa smiled back at me.

We were about ten miles down the river from the village when Papa said it was time to drop the anchor.

"Is it time to put the poles in the water?" I asked.

"Yes, go ahead and drop the anchor, but remember not to splash it so you don't scare the fish. Why don't you swing your pole over in that spot," Papa said. But as I swung my pole, I got too close, and my hook caught his neck.

"Oh! You've hooked me! You got me good – and deep too. Oh my goodness! Don't pull it – it's really deep!" he warned.

"Oh, Papa, I am so sorry! What do I do?" I pleaded.

"First of all, stay calm and sit down before you fall into the river and me with you," Papa said. "Now carefully put the pole down and open the tackle box. There's a pair of wire cutters in there. Do you see them?" Papa said.

"Yes, I see them," I said.

"Zualoo, you are going to have to help me get the hook out because I cannot see it," Papa said.

"But Papa, I don't want to hurt you even more than I already have!" I said, trembling.

"Honey, it's okay," he comforted. "I'll hold the torch, and all you have to do is clip the hook in half and I'll slide the pieces out."

"Oh, Papa, I'm scared!" I wailed.

"If you don't do this it could get infected, and you know it's three days to the nearest village doctor," said Papa evenly.

"Okay, I will do it," I said. As I began to clip the hook, I noticed Papa's shirt was soaked in blood. I wanted to faint but began to pray and ask God for help.

"Dear God, please help me not to be afraid and to be strong and trust in you," I whispered. Before I knew it, the hook snapped free in the cutters! Papa gave a big yelp and it was over.

"Papa, I'm so sorry. Did it hurt that bad?" I nervously asked.

"Well... Have you ever had your top lip pulled over your whole head?" Papa joked.

"Ah, well, not really," I said with a furrowed brow.

"Neither have I, but that's what it felt like," he said, trying to keep a straight face.

Then Papa burst out laughing. I wasn't sure if I should cry or laugh, but then I started laughing with him. Papa quickly backed the hook out, and I handed him a rag. By this time, his shirt was too soaked in blood to wear, and it really attracted a lot of mosquitos.

"Hand me my sack, Zualoo, so I can change my shirt," Papa said. As he was putting on a dry shirt, I began washing the bloody one in the river so it wouldn't attract mosquitos.

"No, no, don't do that! The blood will bring the piranhas, and you know what that means," he warned.

I knew exactly what it meant. It meant that the piranhas would scare away the Tiger Fish. But it was too late. We could already see their shiny reflection in the water from the torches. No fish tonight for the village. My head sunk to my chest. Not only did I injure my father, I also ruined tonight's fishing trip. Papa put his arm around me and gave me a big hug.

"It's okay. We all make mistakes. Don't worry about it. We'll just pull up anchor and coast awhile until we get downriver a few miles. Maybe there will be fewer mosquitos too. The night is still young," Papa comforted.

"Okay," I said with my head down. Papa always had a way of smoothing things over and not making people feel bad for their mistakes.

Chapter 3

A Creepy Night

We cruised for about an hour when we noticed that the wildlife started to become unusually loud. In fact, the frogs and crickets got louder and louder the further downstream we went. It was almost like they were trying to tell us something – but what?

"Zualoo, go to the right. Let's take that branch of the river," Papa said.

"But we've never been that way before. Are you sure?" I questioned.

He nodded. "Let's coast for a little while down this way. Maybe we'll find a spot where it's not so noisy," he said hopefully.

"Okay," I nodded back and steered the boat in that direction.

After another hour, Papa said to drop anchor.

"This is probably a good place," Papa pointed.

"I'll be sure not to splash the anchor," I said.

"Good. Now gently put your pole in the water and bring the big one in," Papa instructed.

"Is your neck still bleeding?" I asked, glancing sideways at his neck.

"No, but it hurts pretty badly," Papa said. Just as he said that, I felt a jerk on my pole.

"Papa, I got a bite!" I exclaimed.

"You know what to do! Just keep your pole still, and when it jerks again, set the hook," Papa coached.

"Yeah, I know," I said excitedly.

Once again I felt something on my pole, but it wasn't a jerk like before. This time my pole just started to bend in half.

"I think I have something this time, Papa, and it feels like he is bigger than me. Help me! I don't think I can bring him in by myself," I said as I grunted and pulled.

"Here, let me hold the pole with you and we'll bring him in together. Just don't jerk it or the line will break," Papa said, quickly taking over the pole. As we pulled and pulled, I asked Papa how much he thought it weighed.

"I don't know, honey, just keep pulling!" he said through clenched teeth.

Papa was a very strong man, and I had never seen him struggle with a fish like this one. As we heard the pole starting to snap, Papa exclaimed, "I think I see him! Get the net!"

As I started to put the net towards the fish, I realized that it would be of no use because whatever we caught was so huge that it wouldn't fit in the net.

"What is it, Papa? It's huge! Will it even fit in the boat?" I yelled.

Papa continued to struggle and was out of breath as he said, "I don't know, but I think it will feed our village for six months. Grab the torch so we can get a better look at it."

As Papa finally got it close to the boat, we saw with dismay that the torch revealed that it was just a huge log. Papa and I looked at each other, huffing and puffing and out of breath. Then we both sat down exhausted and laughed. We couldn't believe it.

"Well, Zualoo, we may not catch anything tonight, but we sure are having fun," he stated, chuckling.

"But I did catch you," I added, grinning. "Hey, have you noticed something, Papa?"

"What's that?" he said.

"Now it's dead quiet. I don't even hear one peeper frog or anything. First we could hardly hear each other talk a while ago and now it's just silence," I whispered.

"You're right, Zualoo. I've never experienced a night like this. It's quite strange," Papa said thoughtfully.

A thick fog started to roll in, and it was starting to feel really creepy. The beads of sweat on my forehead began to actually feel cold.

"Papa, I don't feel like fishing anymore. Can we go home?" I asked nervously.

"If we don't bring the village any fish home tonight, we don't eat tomorrow."

"I know, but I'm willing to starve tomorrow. I just want to get out of here," I begged.

"I'll make a deal. Let's fish for another thirty minutes, and then we will head home," Papa bargained.

"Deal," I said.

Chapter 4

All Overboard

"Papa, I want to be just like you when I grow up," I said with a big smile. He didn't seem to be afraid of the night or the fog or the eerie silence.

Papa smiled too. "That's nice, honey, but there really isn't anything to be afraid of out here."

Just then my fishing pole bent almost in half again, and whatever was on the line nearly pulled me into the water. Papa caught hold of me just as I was headed into the deep.

"What was that?" I gasped as Papa quickly pulled up his own line into the boat.

"I don't know, but my heart skipped a beat or two," Papa said.

When I pulled up my line, there was a nice-sized Goliath fish on my line, but it was bitten in half.

"What do you think could have done that?" I asked as I studied the fish.

"I don't know." He stroked his chin. "It's very unusual. A lot of strange things are going on tonight," he said thoughtfully.

As our eyes were fixed on the half-eaten fish and we tried to figure out what it could mean, a deafening roar bellowed behind us in the dark. We were immediately thrown into the water as a huge wave tossed our boat upside-down.

"Zualoo! Where are you?" Papa shouted as he surfaced.

"Here, Papa! I'm over here! Can you see me?" I yelled back, splashing frantically in the dark.

"No! I'll keep talking, and you swim towards my voice!" Papa yelled back.

As I swam towards him, I felt something rub across my right leg.

"Papa! Papa!" I screamed.

"Zualoo! What is it?!" Papa screamed back.

"Something is in the water! Help me!" I yelled, terrified.

"Swim faster! Come to me!" Papa shouted.

I finally reached Papa's arms, and we swam to the shore as fast as we could.

"Are you okay? Do you think it was a crocodile?" Papa sat me down and checked me for injuries. I was so out of breath I could hardly speak.

"Well, I thought it was at first, but it was too long to be a crocodile 'cause it rubbed down my leg like it was a long tree trunk. Where is Poppy?" I yelled out her name, fearing she may have drowned.

"She probably swam downriver. We'll just have to find her later. Dogs have a good sense of direction, so I'm sure she will find her way home." Papa assured.

We sat on the shore while we caught our breath, but we needed to find shelter quickly as it was starting to rain.

"Can you hand me that big stick behind you, the one with the crooked end? I'll make a torch so we can see to find shelter for the night," Papa said.

"But how will we light it?" I said, realizing that our supply of hakonish was floating down the river with everything else.

"That's a good question, and here," he said with a flourishing motion, "is your answer."

Papa reached into his fishing sack and pulled out his special fire starter that Mama made him as a wedding present. Mama is a very gifted woman and had learned how to make the starter from her father. You can easily start a fire with it by striking two special rocks together and making a spark. Papa quickly wrapped some tree moss around the head of the stick. Much to our relief, he had also packed some extra hakonish.

"Here, Zualoo, you know what to do, but be careful," he warned.

"Yes, Papa," I said.

As I struck the one rock called *chim chim* against the other rock called *hiluki*, sparks began to fly, and we were able to make a torch to search for firewood. I also stuffed my shirt with a lot of moss so we could use it later to add to the torch. It was good fire starter too.

"Let's see if we can find some shelter for the night," Papa said, holding out his hand.

We had walked through the dense jungle for only a few minutes when Papa put his hand on my shoulder.

"Look! Over there!" Papa pointed to something about 60 yards away.

"Yeah, I see it. Is that what I think it is?" I asked.

"It's a cave," Papa affirmed.

I was so excited because I had never been in a cave before and neither had Papa. We had just heard stories of caves being in other parts of the world, but didn't think there were any in Africa. I gripped Papa's hand tightly as we approached the opening.

"Papa, what if there are dangerous animals inside?" I looked up at him nervously.

"Well, that's a chance we'll have to take. It's a perfect place to spend the night. Remember, God is with us, so let's trust him," Papa said.

Chapter Five

Writing On The Wall

We gathered some dry wood to build a fire as quickly as we could before the torch went out. As we approached the entrance of the cave, we began to smell a strange odor that reeked like rotten eggs and made us want to throw up. But after we went inside a little ways, we couldn't smell it any more.

"Here, this looks like a good place to build a fire," Papa said.

It didn't take us long to get a blaze going, and as we sat warming ourselves, I asked Papa how he was able to hold onto his fishing sack after being thrown in the water.

"I just felt like I should tie it around my waist after we were done fighting that fish. I never do that, so I believe God put it in my mind to do so, don't you?" he asked.

I nodded.

"Why don't you pray and ask him to continue to do that and help us get back home tomorrow," Papa said.

"Lord," I prayed, "please keep us safe through the night and get us back home. We believe you can do that. Amen," I finished. "Papa, I'm really hungry. Got anything in that fishing sack to eat?" I said.

"No, but I do have my knife that will help us catch our breakfast in the morning. If you go to sleep you won't be hungry anymore," he suggested.

"Okay," I agreed and found myself yawning. "I love you. Goodnight."

"I love you too, honey. Goodnight."

As I lay down on the hard floor of the cave, I used the moss for a pillow, not knowing that the next morning I would be sorry I did because I would have tiny bugs in my hair and clothes. While looking up at the fire flickering on the ceiling, I saw what looked like blinking stars. I knew they couldn't be starts, though, because we weren't outside.

"Papa, what is that?" I whispered. He looked up to the ceiling of the cave to where I was gazing.

"Oh, those must be the reflections of bat eyes. I've heard that they love to live in caves. They won't hurt you, and they are actually a blessing because they love to eat mosquitos," he said.

Even though the bats made me nervous as they hung above us, I knew that God was with us, and Papa had made me feel at peace because he didn't look worried. His confidence in the Lord helped me fall asleep quickly. No sooner did I shut my eyes did I wake up to the most delicious smell: a fire and roasted rabbit!

"You going to sleep all morning? Let's get those bones moving! We gotta eat and get going!" Papa said, turning the rabbit on the spit.

"Mmmm, it smells so good!" My stomach rumbled, and I crouched by the fire, sniffing. "How were you able to catch and cook a rabbit so fast and without waking me up?" I asked.

"Well, I guess I'm just a good hunter like my papa was," he winked and gingerly took a piece of hot juicy meat off of the spit and handed it to me.

"And a good cook, too," I said as I licked my fingers. "This is delicious!"

While we were eating, I noticed the sound of distantly running water deeper into the cave and asked Papa if he heard it as well.

"Yes, I do, and I think it would be a good idea to see where it is coming from. We could both wash up a bit in it, and perhaps it is good to drink," he suggested.

After our quick breakfast, we put out the fire, but not before making a good torch to see where we were going in the cave. We headed straight for the source of the noise, and it didn't take us long to find a small stream flowing through the cave.

"Hold this while I wash up, and then I'll taste the water," Papa said.

As he handed me the torch, I noticed what looked like drawings on the wall behind him.

"Papa, look behind you!" I gasped, pointing.

His eyes widened when he saw my shocked expression. "What is it?" he asked, frozen.

"Turn around and you will see!" I said, continuing to point.

As he did, he let out a long, "Woww, look at that!"

"What is this?" I asked, walking over to the cave's wall and trailing my finger along the faint outlines.

"It's true! It's really true!" he softly muttered to himself.

"Huh? What do you mean?" I watched Papa gaze at the outlines, shaking his head in amazement.

"These are cave drawings made by people that lived a very long time ago. Look here," he pointed to a drawing. "You can see how they lived and what was important to them."

There were many drawings on the wall: tools, corn, wheat, a village with several huts, and some children playing with a dog. There was also an enormously tall creature with a long tail and sharp teeth. It towered over the huts and was breathing out fire.

"What is that?" I asked Papa, pointing to the creature.

"That is exactly what caught my attention right away. It looks like a dinosaur that is being hunted for food." Papa put his finger on what looked like a hunter with a knife in his hand, but when he scraped off some mold around the knife it eventually became a long spear.

"What is a dinosaur?" I said curiously. I had never heard that word.

"It's a creature that lived thousands of years ago in Noah's day," Papa began.

"You mean the Noah in God's book?" I asked.

"That's right! Did you know that God made these creatures on the same day as Adam and Eve? And a man named Job wrote of one he called "behemoth". Job doesn't call it a dinosaur, but he describes a creature that moved its tail like a cedar tree and his bones were like iron. So it must have been something like this drawing," he explained.

"Wow, that's awesome!" I said. "But I just have one question. You said they lived a very long time ago, so how do you know they aren't alive today? If God told Noah to put two of each kind of animal on the ark, he did, right? And that means he would have had to put these creatures on the ark too, right? And if they got on the ark, they must have gotten off. So why couldn't they be alive today?"

"I thought you said you had one question!" Papa winked at me, and we both laughed. "Well, Zualoo, you've brought up some interesting thoughts."

"I have another thought. If Noah's flood covered the whole earth, does that mean this cave was formed while the waters were sloshing around?" I asked, looking around the cave.

"Mm-hmm," Papa agreed.

"So that means that these drawings were made after Noah's flood!" I exclaimed.

"Great observation, Zualoo! I guess that means we can't really say dinosaurs are all gone. But I've never seen a dinosaur, have you?" he chuckled as I shook my head.

After a quick wash-up, Papa cupped his hands and took a drink to see if it was good.

"Mmm," he murmured. "It's good! Go ahead, honey."

After we drank our bellies full, I asked Papa if we could explore the cave and perhaps find another way out so we didn't have to go by that awful smell where we came in.

"Sure, but stay close to me. We don't know what lurks around the next corner."

Chapter Six

Left Alone

We followed the stream in hopes that it would lead us to another exit. But going through the twists and turns was a challenge for both of us, especially for Papa who was a heavy man and had to rest more than me. As we went further down into the cave, we noticed our voices were echoing more and more until we found ourselves in a huge room with an enormous lake in it. It was amazing that a lake could be in a cave, but there it was.

"Papa, do you think there are any fish in it? I'm really hungry," I said.

"Me, too. Let's take a look," Papa said. We both watched the water for a while to see if there was any movement, but it was very still.

"Zualoo, hand me some of the rabbit pieces I gave you. We'll throw some into the lake and see if any fish go after it," Papa said.

I paused and made a face of disappointment as I told him that I forgot to put them in my shirt pouch back at the fire.

"Zualoo! What am I going to do with you? You will have to stay here while I go back to get them," he instructed.

"In the dark? By myself? Papa!" I wailed.

"I won't be gone long, and there is nothing in this cave that will hurt you," Papa said.

I watched him as he started finding his way back to the campfire until I couldn't see any more light from the torch. It was so dark I couldn't even see my hand in front of my face. While I waited at the water's edge for Papa to return, there was nothing to do but ponder the events since we left home. So much had happened, and I wondered if God had planned all of this out this way for a reason. I tried to keep my mind on Papa getting back to me quickly because I was really afraid to be alone.

"God, help Papa to be careful and to hurry back. And help me not to be afraid," I prayed. The moment I said "Amen", I heard the sound like water making waves and hitting the rocks. Then I heard a very deep sound like someone belching.

"Is that you, Papa? Papa?!" I called, trying desperately to peer into the dark.

I was looking toward the direction where I thought he had gone out, but the sounds were behind me. My hair stood up, and I got goose bumps all over my body when I heard another deep belching sound. Then the whole cave lit up like a flash of lightning for a brief second.

"Papa! Papa!" I screamed.

No answer. I quickly crawled behind a big boulder that I saw during the brief flash of light. I put my hand over my mouth to keep from screaming again. Thoughts ran through my mind as tears filled my eyes. Is something in the water? What was that light? Is Papa coming back? Am I going to die alone in the dark? Will my family never see me again? I began to shake uncontrollably and cold sweat ran down my spine as I prayed again that God would protect me and Papa.

Then I saw the cave starting to light up slowly and heard Papa yelling my name in the distance. I didn't want to respond until he got a little closer since I didn't know what was around me. As soon as Papa got a few feet from me I leaped from behind the rock and into his arms, weeping.

"Papa, why were you gone so long? I was so scared," I sobbed.

"I got lost for a few minutes. But I did get some rabbit to fish with. See?" He patted his pouch. "Why were you so scared? I said there is nothing in this cave that will harm you," he soothed.

"Papa, I think there is something in the water, and I saw a light flash behind me, too," I said.

"Oh, good! Maybe there are fish in the water after all. Here, hold the torch while I make a spear," he instructed.

He fished around in his sack and pulled out an arrowhead. He took the long stick we found at the river and used one of his shoelaces to tie the arrowhead to.

"Now hold the torch over there, and I'll throw some bits of rabbit in the water. But be very still so you don't scare them," he said.

We threw some of the rabbit in the water, but nothing ever came close to the water's edge. We were just about to give up trying when we noticed waves beginning to come towards our feet.

"Papa, that's what I was trying to tell you. I was sitting right here when I heard waves and then a low belching noise before the whole cave lit up," I warned.

"Look. What's that?" Papa said, pointing to what looked like a small animal swimming very fast all around the lake.

"I don't know, Papa, but let's hide behind that rock and watch it," I pleaded, tugging on his arm.

As we kept our eyes on the animal, it got bigger and bigger until we realized it was not a small animal. We were only looking at the top of its head. It rose out of the water, as big as a house. It was a dinosaur!

"Ahhhhhh!" we both screamed, and Papa covered my mouth as it turned its head and looked in our direction.

Chapter Seven

Stuck

We quickly extinguished the torch so it would not see us. The creature let out a long bellowing roar, and then another.

"Keep your voice down," Papa whispered in my ear, his hand still clamped over my mouth.

I nodded my head with wide eyes, and then he took his hand away from my mouth. I could not see Papa, but he held my hand tightly. The creature roared a third time and then belched right before lighting up the cave for a moment.

"Papa," I whispered. "That's what I was trying to tell you! Hey!" I whispered excitedly, remembering. "The drawing on the wall – the dinosaur!"

"Yes, Zualoo, they are still alive! They are still alive!" he hissed.

"Noah did put them on the ark, didn't he? What are we going to do?" I asked, my mind racing.

"Wait till he blows fire again and look for the path back to where we came in. We'll crawl as far as we can until he blows some more. Hopefully he'll keep doing that until we can get far enough away where he can't reach us," he planned.

We noticed that after the dinosaur belched, it would click its teeth and then breathe out fire. So we timed it just right and moved a few feet more each time. We could hear him sniffing and figured out it was the rabbit pieces I still had left in my pouch, so I threw some in his direction to distract the creature while we scooted away. I stayed right next to Papa and held onto his shirt as we crawled and finally made it into a tight place where we could rest and were safe.

We waited and waited for what seemed liked hours for the thing to go away but it just kept sniffing, belching, and blowing fire. Between each of its fiery displays, we could hear our stomachs growling which didn't encourage the creature to go away as we figured that it could hear our stomachs too. Finally, it sank back under the water so we didn't have to whisper anymore.

"Papa, do you think he lives in this cave?" I asked.

"Yeah, he probably does. But I don't want to live here with him, do you?" Papa joked. I shook my head in a vigorous no. "Let's try to get back to the entrance. Just hold on to me. We'll follow the stream in that direction," Papa said.

We couldn't see a thing since "Mokee", as I named him, had disappeared. So Papa just kept his hand in the stream and we crawled inch by inch on our bellies. Our knees and hands were getting scraped and bloody and our heads were repeatedly bumping into rocks, so we rested and took a drink from the stream.

"Thank God for this stream, huh, Papa?" I said.

"Amen to that," he agreed.

I gasped.

"What? What is it? Did something crawl on you?" Papa exclaimed.

"Something did rub on my leg," I replied, thinking.

"Was it a snake?" Papa asked.

"No, I mean in the river. I just thought of something. You said that the creature that Job described had a tail like a cedar tree. Remember? A tree trunk is what I said I thought rubbed against my leg after we were thrown in the river! Papa, it could have been this dinosaur!" I said, wide-eyed.

"Well, you don't really know if that's what it was. But you are still alive, so let's be thankful for that," he said.

By now our stomachs were making such a racket that we had our own little concert going on.

"Are you ready to eat something?" Papa asked.

"Ready? I was ready two hours ago. You mean you've got something hidden in that sack of yours? Papa, have you been holding out on me?" I teased.

"Not at all," Papa said.

"Well, what are we going to eat? Your other shoelace?" I teased again.

Papa responded, "No, we are going to eat fish."

"Fish? We didn't catch anything, remember?" I said.

"You're right. So we will now," Papa said.

"Huh?" I questioned.

"You may not like this, but give me your hand," Papa said.

"You are scaring me already," I said. Papa gently put my hand in the water and I immediately felt some tiny fish nibbling at my fingers.

"Now try to catch some for us to eat," Papa said.

"You mean this is lunch?" I said.

"Yep," Papa said.

"Raw!? Alive!?" I squealed.

"Yep!" he replied.

"That's gross!" I moaned.

"Oh, well. I guess you'll be hungry for a while longer. But at least try to catch me some," Papa said.

"Okay, but I'm not eating any," I stated.

To my surprise, I managed to catch some of the inch-long fish and gave them to Papa. I felt around for Papa's arm and gently placed the fish in his cupped hand.

"Here, you go. Would you like a cup of tea with that, sir?" I joked. Papa chuckled and the next thing I heard was a slurp, crunch, and "ahhh".

"Oh, I'm going to throw up!" I said.

"But what are you going to throw up? You haven't eaten anything," Papa said.

We both giggled. We just couldn't believe we had been through so much in the short time since leaving home. Now we were in a dark cave eating raw fish, and we didn't even know what it looked like. I did finally eat some because I was so hungry, but I didn't slurp them between my lips. I just popped them in my mouth and swallowed them without crunching. I could feel them swimming down my throat. Each time I would gag, wanting to throw them back up, but the little guys stayed down. After our meal of the slimy unknown, we got on our hands and knees to get moving again.

Suddenly, Papa yelped, "Oh, my back! My back!"

"What's wrong, Papa?"

"I can't move. I twisted my back. I guess all this twisting and turning and sitting has cramped my back. Ohhh," he moaned.

"What should I do? Can I massage it? Maybe I can work it out," I said hopefully.

"I guess. Just take it easy," he agreed.

I tried to work out the cramps, but he just couldn't move.

"Zualoo, I think you are going to have to find your way back home," Papa said.

"Oh, Papa, not again. I just can't be by myself again! I can't leave you here alone. What if the dinosaur comes back and finds you?" I said with dismay. I curled up to Papa's chest and started to cry.

"It will be okay. Mokee couldn't get to me if he wanted to. And you'll be alright. Have faith. I believe God put us on this journey for a reason, and I have a suspicion that he will see both of us through," he replied.

"But Papa, how am I going to see to get out?" I asked.

"Just keep your hand in the water, remember? It will lead you to the entrance," Papa said. "Let's pray once more before you leave. I'll pray this time." He took my hand and began, "Heavenly Father, we know you love us and are watching over us. Please keep me safe in this cave and help Zualoo get home safe too. Amen." He squeezed my hand. "Zualoo, take the torch and fire rocks to use later."

"I will not be afraid, Papa. I know God is with me. I will be brave too, so don't you worry about me," I said, more bravely than I felt. I gave him a big hug and told him I loved him before leaving for my lonely adventure in the dark.

Chapter Eight

Fear To Tears

As I set out, I was determined to keep the entrance of the cave on my mind and not on my troubles so I would remain brave. It seemed to take forever to crawl back to where we had built a fire, but I finally made it and could now see to get out of the cave.

When I did, I was greeted by a glorious day, and I didn't even care about that stinking egg smell near the entrance, whatever it was. I quickly ran to the river and knew immediately to follow the water's edge upstream towards home. Before I set out, I glanced downstream and saw a wonderful sight: our boat! It didn't go downriver very far, as it was caught in the branches of an enormous tree that had fallen into the water.

"Thank you, Lord!" I said out loud.

The tree was so wide, I thought all I would need to do was carefully walk on it down to where the boat was – but no such luck. It was covered with a thick, slippery moss, so I got back on my belly once again. I grabbed a sharp, thin rock and began scraping the moss off the bark ahead of me. It came off fairly easy. The tree was about 40 feet long, but I knew I had to get our boat, so I kept plugging away at it. At about the halfway point, I had to take a break because my back was starting to cramp. So I lay there on my stomach, thinking about Papa and how to get help from my village family who, for all they knew, thought we were having an extra-long fishing trip.

My mind began to race. Would they believe us? After all, how could so much happen to two people in such a short amount of time? And discovering a dinosaur? Surely everyone would think that we were just making up an adventurous campfire story for a good laugh.

While laying still and pondering all this, my eye caught some movement across the river in the distance. It was Mokee! *Oh no!* I thought. *What if he sees me?* I lay very still as I watched it eating a huge Goliath Tiger Fish. My heart was pounding so hard as I tried to figure out what I should do. If I moved he would surely see me, and I didn't know if I could outrun the beast. The only thing I could do was to lay still and hope he would go away. I closed my eyes and whispered a prayer.

When I opened my eyes the next moment, I couldn't believe it. Mokee was gone! I wanted to shout in relief, but then I wondered… Where did he go? Should I move or wait a few minutes? Maybe he was still around and I couldn't see him. I focused my eyes on an object in the distance so that I could see if something moved.

Minutes ticked by, and I began to relax. Surely he had moved on.

Splash! Roaaar!

Mokee's long neck burst up out of the water just a few feet from me! I immediately wanted to scream, and my heart felt like it was going to burst. But out of instinct and partly out of terror, I froze, not even moving an eye. The scaly, wet dinosaur began to sniff around, its nose coming inches from my face, a deep growl coming from his throat.

"Lord, don't let it eat me, don't let it eat me, *don't let it eat meeee*!" I prayed.

A rustle came from the boat, and Mokee stretched his neck over to see what it was. As soon as he got to the boat, Poppy popped up from the boat's helm and began to bark! Poppy was in the boat the whole time since we had been tossed out!

I remained immobile as I watched Poppy bravely stand down the dinosaur. As big as the creature was, it was mind-boggling that it cowered away from the dog. The confrontation only lasted a few minutes when Poppy bit one of its legs, and Mokee slunk back into the water and swam away with its head, back, and tail sticking up.

"Poppy. Poppy!" I whispered. She looked all around but didn't see me until I stuck my head up.

"Poppy, stay girl. I'm coming," I motioned. Her tail wagged furiously, but she stayed in the boat. She looked muddy and hungry, and waited patiently until I was able to crawl to her in the boat.

"Poppy, you saved me!" I said as I scratched her back and threw my arms around her.

The boat was caught on a tree limb that I was able to break off easily. I pulled the boat onto land as far as I could and tied it to a stump. I would have to get it later since I didn't have any paddles.

"Come on, Poppy. Let's go," I said, and turned to face upriver.

Chapter Nine

Growl Behind Us

As we started to head home, I reasoned that the river must somehow join with the lake inside the cave. How else could Mokee get into the cave since the opening was only big enough for a person to get through? Poppy and I were both so excited to be on our way together that we ran as fast as we could, staying close to the river. The sun was in our face, and it was a scorcher of a day.

After running and walking for about three hours, we had to stop and take a drink from the river. It didn't taste too great, especially compared to the clean cave water, but it was refreshing and rejuvenated us. While we rested for a few minutes, I sensed that something was watching us. Poppy sensed it too, and the hair on her back stood up. It became very quiet, and then we heard a noise behind us. I suddenly got very nervous. I slowly turned around to see what it was and yelped when a rabbit popped out of the bushes.

"Poppy, no!" I said as she quickly chased after it. I didn't want her to leave me all alone, but I couldn't blame her because I knew she was hungry. Maybe she'd save some for me too. I decided to stay where I was rather than go search for her and hoped that she would come back to the same spot.

As I waited in the shade, I again got the same feeling that something was still watching me, so I moved to hide in a bush just in case something was out there lurking. The bush was full of thorns, so I figured maybe that would keep any dangerous animals away. I sighed. Would this adventure ever be over? What would be next?

I watched a black-headed Hoopoe land right in front of me to feed her baby chicks. I didn't notice the nest when I entered the bush, and when the bird saw me, she started making deafening, squawking sounds. So much for trying to hide from whatever was in the forest.

After a while the Hoopoe flew away, so I looked into the nest to take a peek at the chicks. What I found instead were five blue eggs she was trying to protect. As much as I wanted her to hatch them, my stomach was pinching with hunger, so I plucked the eggs from the nest, hoping that the eggs were still fluid. I thought about how unhappy she would be when she got back to an empty nest, but I knew she would start again somewhere else. Gently, I cracked open the end of an egg and found that thankfully it was still fluid. I then sucked out the juices of four of the eggs, trying not to think about it. Before I ate the fifth, I decided to save it for Poppy in case she didn't catch the rabbit.

I couldn't sit in the thorn bush forever, so I carefully maneuvered my way out, getting only a minor scratch on my cheek. As I began to call out for Poppy as I walked up the river toward home, I realized that I had never been in this area of the jungle before and didn't think anyone from my village had either. I figured that's why none of us had ever seen Mokee. The further I walked up stream, the higher the shoreline grew until I was about 30 feet above the river. It was a great place to call out for Poppy. I called repeatedly, but she did not appear.

"Please bring Poppy back to me. I need her to help me get home," I prayed.

The temperature was steadily rising, and I was drenched with sweat. My stomach was in knots, probably complaining about the uncooked bird eggs, the raw fish, the dirty river water, and the heat. I sat down near a ledge to rest for a couple of minutes and called again for Poppy.

Looking into the river from my lofty vantage point, I noticed something I'd never seen before. There were lots of fish jumping out of the water in one large area. While I enjoyed this curious site, I heard a growl behind me and knew instantly it was a large cat. I looked around for something to throw at him and squatted down to pick up a rock. I could hear him getting closer as he stepped on dry leaves and twigs, so I slowly turned around. I threw the rock as hard as I could.

Bullseye!

The rock hit him square in the nose, and he yowled furiously. He bolted towards me and leaped into the air toward my face.

At the same time, Poppy burst from the underbrush and knocked me flat on my back. The jungle cat flew over me and fell flailing into the river below right where the fish were jumping. The next thing we saw was Mokee's head crest up out of the water and his enormous body chase after the unfortunate cat.

I sat up and hugged Poppy, still shivering with the suddenness of it all. I reached in my pocket to feed her the last egg I was saving for her, but unfortunately it got smashed when she knocked me over. It probably didn't matter to her, though. She looked like she did indeed catch the rabbit, as her face was covered in what looked like a fresh kill.

Poppy and I continued to trek our way home, but we only had another hour before dark. With all that had happened during the day, we had really been slowed down. We would have to spend yet another night in the jungle away from home, but at least this time I had my dog to keep me company and protect me.

As we walked in the direction of our village, I picked up some wood to build a fire near the shoreline. I realized that Mokee could still be around, but I just had to give my fears to God and keep my mind on Papa and home.

"Here, Poppy, this is a good spot. We'll make camp here," I told her.

I wasn't able to find enough wood for a big fire, but there was enough to make several torches which would last us during the warm night. Besides, we didn't have anything to cook over the fire anyway.

No sooner did we light the torch did a thunderstorm roll in. Luckily and quickly, we were able to find a Kapok tree for shelter from the rain. This one was huge and happened to have a hollowed-out trunk, so we stayed mostly dry and were able to keep the torch burning.

Thankfully, the storm was short-lived, but on the downside, it brought out the mosquitos. I certainly didn't want to get bit, so the only choice I had was to take some of the hakonish and rub it all over my face and body that was exposed. It really made me stink, so nothing came near me, not even Poppy.

As we settled in for a long night, I prayed, "I ask you again to please keep Papa safe, and us too. Help us to get back home tomorrow. Amen. And, oh, please help us find some food tomorrow to give us strength. Amen again."

I put out the torch, and Poppy finally decided to curl up next to me as if she wanted to pray with me. We shut our eyes, and because we were both so exhausted, we fell asleep almost instantly.

Chapter Ten

Eaten Alive

It hadn't been that long since we had fallen asleep when Poppy woke me up, barking ferociously at something in the river. Was it Mokee? Was it that cat?

I decided to light another torch and use it to defend myself. When the light flared up, I could see that it was Mokee, coming right at us.

"Ahhh!" I screamed. "Ahhhhh!!"

This was it, I thought. I am going to die.

Mokee had me cornered against the Kapok tree. I could not move. I just kept screaming and Poppy kept barking to scare the beast away, but it kept coming closer. Poppy leaped out and sunk her teeth into its long tail, but with one swing, Mokee threw Poppy against a tree. I heard her yelp and fall limp to the ground, dead.

Mokee was distracted by Poppy, and I took off running. I threw the torch down so it wouldn't attract Mokee to me, but it was no use. The creature caught up with me and latched onto my leg with its large teeth and began swinging me like a rag doll in the air. I'd never felt such pain in my life. I hoped he would just eat me whole and let it be over quickly. But he kept swinging me like he wanted to play before gulping me down.

Then, with one quick jerk, it swung me high in the air above its head. As I began falling back down toward its wide-open jaws, I closed my eyes and prayed that I would die instantly. The next thing I felt was its sticky tongue on my face and could feel its sharp teeth in my back...

My eyes flew open, and I woke up to Poppy licking the sweat off my face and the Kapok tree poking me in the back. Realizing it had all been a nightmare, I began to weep like a baby, joyful that we were both still alive. Even in my sleep, we couldn't seem to escape the terrifying dinosaur.

I couldn't go to sleep after that, so I kept the torch going and listened to my stomach growl for hours. As the sun began to finally rise and give me enough light to walk by, Poppy and I set out once more.

We were both absolutely starving and looked for anything that moved to catch and eat. I didn't care if I had to eat it alive. At least we had plenty of water to drink from the river. As we peeked over a small hill, something caught my eye.

"Look, Poppy, a Strangler fig!" I exclaimed. "Hallelujah! Thank you, Lord. You answered last night's prayer! We can eat now, girl,." I said to Poppy.

The Strangler fig tree is not only a favorite of humans, but animals love it too. We ate till we just couldn't take another bite, and I loaded Papa's fishing sack full for later. Now we had enough strength to make some good time, so we ran and ran and ran, following the river upstream towards home.

We knew we were getting close to the village because we could smell something cooking and then saw the smoke in the distant sky. We also started recognizing the area as we saw some of our hunting spots in the trees. Poppy started barking loudly as we approached the village, and everyone came running out to greet us.

"Zualoo! What happened? Where's your papa?" Mama exclaimed.

"Mama, too much has happened to explain it all right now. Papa is hurt and in a cave. I'll show the way to him, but we must hurry," I said.

After getting some nourishment for me and Poppy, my two uncles loaded another sack with food for Papa, and we all set out to rescue him. Poppy came, too.

We had plenty of light as we launched the boat from the shore. I explained as much as I could to my uncles, but they just stared at each other in disbelief and horror, especially when I told them about Mokee.

"Zualoo, how can a small girl like you have gone through so much and still be alive?" my uncle Shemoa marveled.

"I don't know, but Papa and I did a lot of praying and God did a lot of answering. Let's pray that Papa is still alive," I suggested.

So Uncle Shemoa did just that and asked God to help us. We paddled as fast as we could down the river as I tried to locate the boat.

"Zualoo, where are you taking us? We have never been this far down the river. It is forbidden territory," Uncle Taokinu said.

"Forbidden? What do you mean?" I asked.

Uncle Taokinu pointed to a very large bolder and said, "Do you see that? It has our mark on it with a line and then on the other side it has the mark of the Uganla tribe. That means neither of the tribes are to cross into each other's territory or it could mean war."

I realized that Papa and I never saw it because it was so dark that night. We went right by it. Now I understood why our village never went to that area.

"Well, what are we going to do? We have to find Papa!" I was starting to get upset.

"I'm sorry, Zualoo. We must turn back. We cannot risk war. We will have a meeting with the chief and elders tonight to decide what to do," Uncle Taokinu said.

I fell down at his feet and began to beg and cry that we go on, but he and Uncle Shemoa turned the boat around. After all that I went through to get help, and now we were turning back. I just couldn't believe it. God answered all my other prayers. Why was he not answering my biggest one – to get Papa home?

"Mama, what do you think the elders are going to do?" I asked later as we sat in the distance watching the men talk around the fire.

"I'm not sure, my love, but we need to be prepared to accept whatever they decide, good or bad. They are wise men who trust God," Mama said as she gave me a hug and kissed my head.

"Yes, I know, Mama," I sighed.

It seemed like an eternity while waiting for the men to tell us what they decided, but finally the chief elder walked toward us with a drawn face and eyes looking down.

"The elders have decided to wait until morning. We will send two runners to meet with the Uganla chief for permission to enter his territory," he explained.

"Another night? Another night!?" I exclaimed in frustration. I turned in Mama's lap. "But Mama, Papa is in that cold, dark cave all alone, with no food and probably scared to death."

"I know, honey. I know," she said as she rocked me in her arms and began singing one of my favorite lullabies. Exhaustion overrode frustration, and I fell asleep in her arms.

Chapter Eleven

Bad Shot

I awoke the next day to a wonderful breakfast of *posh posh* and eggs. *Posh posh* is a mixture of corn and karoe root and is very sweet. Mama almost never makes this because the karoe root is very hard to find. I knew she was trying to cheer me up.

As I ate the special breakfast, I watched the elders give orders to the two runners and load the boat with all kinds of peace gifts of food and other valuables.

My nephews, Bachah and Tulu, are twin brothers and not afraid of anything. Between the two of them, they have killed more animals to feed the village than all of the tribe hunters combined. I guess it's because they are so skinny. They can run very fast and climb trees like a monkey.

Tulu and Bachah do everything together: hunt, fish, and always team up for tribal wrestling matches. If one goes somewhere, the other always follows. They love each other like best friends. It's no wonder they were chosen to go meet with the Uganla tribe.

"Zualoo, we are very sorry you cannot go, but we know you will be praying for us. You are so much a prayer warrior," Bachah said as he kissed me on the forehead.

"Yes, I will be praying for you both. Please hurry and come back soon," I said, returning the hug.

"We will bring back good news from the Uganla chief. I know he will let us come back to look for your papa," said Tulu.

I whispered a prayer as I watched them load Poppy onto the canoe and leave.

"Mama, when will they be back? Do you think it will be before dark?" I asked.

"Let's hope so," Mama said, watching the boat leave with worried eyes.

I decided to help Mama with cleaning up the breakfast dishes to get my mind off worrying about the situation, but it was impossible. All I could think about was that cold, dark cave and Papa eating raw, slimy fish. I didn't even know if he was alive.

As Mama and I were finishing up, she tried not to look me in the eyes as we talked, but I noticed that her eyes were watery. She was trying to keep me from crying, but it didn't work because when our eyes connected we both burst into tears. We both hugged each other tightly for a long time.

Between sniffles, I said, "He is alive, Mama, right? I just know he's alive. Papa is so strong," I said, trying to convince myself.

"Zualoo, I think Papa must be alive because he has always been a survivor. Let me tell you a story about him when he was very young," she said.

"Was this before I was born?" I asked.

"Oh, yes, this was when he was a little boy about your age," Mama said.

"You knew Papa when he was my age?" I said with raised eyebrows.

"Yes," Mama said, "I've known your Papa since we were babies. When Papa was about 13 years old, he and I went hunting together. Even as a young boy, he was a very good hunter. He took me with him to teach me how to hunt even though girls didn't do that. I had to sneak away from the elders." She paused, and wagged her finger. "Don't tell Papa I told you this."

"I won't," I whispered with a big smile.

"Well," Mama continued, "in those days, the men would put animal skins on their backs and walk on their hands and knees in the bush to attract other animals of the same kind. When an animal came near, a hunter would shoot arrows at the real one."

"Wasn't that dangerous?" I asked.

"Ahh, yes, very dangerous," she replied. "That's why I'm telling you this story. Papa put on a deer hide and he even had a deer head on. He really looked like a real deer as he pranced around."

"Did you ever get a deer, Mama?" I said with big eyes.

"Well, actually, I did get my first deer that day, but it turned out to be your Papa," Mama said.

"Huh?" I mumbled, puzzled.

"Yep!" She went on. "You see, while I was watching him trying to attract a deer, I noticed he went behind some bushes to the right of me. He was gone so long I figured he was, ahh, let's say watering a bush. While I waited for him I saw a real deer come out from a bush to the left of me. I got so excited that I drew my bow and..." Mama pretended to draw her bow and aim. "...and I shot your Papa right in the thigh!" Mama said.

"But how come you shot Papa? I don't understand. I thought you just said you shot a deer," I said with one squinted eye and protruding lips, trying to picture what she was describing.

"I thought it was a real deer, but what happened was Papa got lost and crawled in a big circle around me. He came out of a bush on the left of me where I was looking for a deer to shoot. And it's a good thing I was a bad shot or Papa would be dead!" Mama said.

"Yeah, good thing," I nodded.

"Well!" Mama continued, "That's only part of the story and not even the worst of it. When I shot your Papa he just happened to be standing in front of a small tree so the arrow pinned him right to it. So he wasn't going anywhere," Mama said.

I just sat and listened with my mouth wide open.

"Papa was in a lot of pain and was losing blood fast. We were both actually scared he was going to die, and we were many miles from the village so no one could hear us yelling for help," Mama said.

My eyes grew big, and I became more serious as Mama continued with the story. "I began praying for God to give me the wisdom to know what to do and the courage to do it. I had to leave Papa all alone and run for help. As a 12-year-old girl, I was scared," she admitted.

My eyes and mouth once again dropped as I said, "Mama, this story sounds like what is happening right now with Papa and me!"

"Yes. Papa seems to get himself in trouble and little girls have to keep rescuing him," Mama exclaimed with a smirk. "Humph!"

"So what happened next?" I asked.

"I had to act quickly, so I said 'Don't go anywhere, I'll be right back.'"

"Oh, Mama, did you really say that to him?" I laughed.

"Yeah," Mama said, remembering with a smile.

"That is so funny!"

"I had to run without stopping and prayed all the way to our village," Mama continued. "When we got back to where Papa was, you'll never guess what we found? He wasn't there! I was terrified! I just knew some wild animals had gotten him. As we looked around for him we saw a blood trail and decided to follow it. But I lagged behind his parents because I didn't want to see what was at the end of the trail.

"My stomach was in knots as we searched for him, and I knew I was in big trouble. I figured I was responsible for his death. Was I going to be sold into slavery? Was I going to have to die too? All kinds of thoughts ran through my head. I just wanted to run away and never go back home," she recalled.

"Ah, Mama, that's sad," I said, rubbing her back. "What did the trail lead to?"

"Well, we followed the trail of blood until we couldn't go any further," she explained.

"You mean there were no more blood drops to follow?" I said with a look of bewilderment.

"No," Mama said, "I mean we came to the end of our territory and the beginning of the Uganla territory."

"You've got to be kidding, Mama. This really sounds way too familiar." I shook my head.

"I know, honey. It really is. Papa knew he wasn't far from the Uganla village, and he realized if he didn't get help from them fast, he would die. So he was able to break off from the tree, but the arrow was still stuck in his thigh," she continued.

"How could he walk to the village then?" I asked. "Did he hop all the way there like a bunny rabbit?" I asked with a smile. Mama smiled and nodded her head yes.

"When we were kids," she continued, "the Uganla tribe was friendly to our people, but because they did not believe in Jehovah God as the only true God, they kept their distance."

"So what happened to Papa when he went to them for help?" I asked.

"As Papa came into their village," Mama continued, "he came right up to the chief's tent and fell down, unconscious.

"Papa told me that the next thing he remembered was that he woke up three days later in the tent of a beautiful, smiling girl who was wiping his sweaty face and feeding him soup. She was the chief's daughter and the most beautiful girl in all the village. And... she wasn't married. The chief had been praying to their gods that she would find a husband soon or she would be cursed and would have to be sacrificed to the gods.

"When Papa came hopping along, the chief just knew his prayers to his gods were answered. For many days, the girl ministered to Papa and fell in love with him. She and the tribe treated him like a king. While he was in bed healing, he could hear sounds of celebration outside the tent each night.

"One night he asked the girl what the music and dance was about, and she told him it was preparation for a wedding. Then Papa asked her who was getting married. She smiled really big and said, 'We are!'

"Papa was bewildered, and he asked her what she meant. She told him she did not like any of the men in her tribe, but her god answered her prayer by sending Papa to her. She told him they would be married as soon as he was able to walk. Papa could not believe his ears!"

"So what did he do? Did they get married?" I asked.

"Hold on, Zualoo," Mama continued. "Papa was determined that he wasn't going to marry the girl no matter how beautiful and kind she was. There were other reasons, too, like the fact that she did not know Jesus as her Savior. And Papa had already decided that someday he was going to marry me."

Mama, paused and commented, "Your Papa has always believed that believers should marry believers. Well, the night before the wedding, Papa told her he would not marry her. He told her she could live with our tribe or stay and be killed. So now I get to tell you who my sister Rowani is."

"Huh?" I said astonished. "You mean Aunt Rowani is that beautiful girl?"

"That's right, Zualoo," Mama whispered. "Rowani chose to run away with your father and join our tribe so she wouldn't have to die. This has been a tribal secret for all of these years and you must keep it in your heart. Do you understand?"

"Yes," I said.

"Good," Mama said, relieved. "You must know that Rowani has had to sacrifice a lot to live with us. She misses her family very much, but she had to leave."

"I understand, Mama," I said, nodding.

As we finished cleaning up, Mama continued. "Papa has also sacrificed much."

"What do you mean?" I asked.

"Papa was told that he if he ever set foot on Uganla territory, he would be killed," she explained. "He heard the chief shouting this as Papa and Rowani were running away."

"Oh no! Papa could be killed!" I realized.

"Zualoo, where is your faith?" Mama replied. "Papa is in God's hands, and he will be alright."

"Yes, I know," I said quietly.

Chapter Twelve

Prisoners

The next morning, I was gently awakened by Mama who told me to get dressed quickly, that I was leaving for a boat trip. Mama looked worried as she helped me pack and gave me breakfast to eat on the way to wherever it was I was going.

As I boarded a canoe, I noticed that all of the men had war paint on and were loading their bows and spears. I knew instantly that we were possibly going to war with the Uganla tribe. But why was I going? Women never went to fight, especially little girls.

As I ate my breakfast, I asked one of the men in my canoe where Tulu was. He reluctantly told me that he was held hostage. Unless I came back to see the Uganla chief, Tulu would die. And then he told me that they had Papa! Papa was alive! I was so happy at first, but then my stomach began to twist as I realized that he could be in grave danger.

Thoughts began to swirl in my head as to why the chief wanted me. As the canoes passed the familiar rock with the tribal writings on them, we began to see some of the Uganla tribesmen along the shoreline. They also had war-painted faces and spears in their hands.

Further down the river, I looked to my left and noticed the cave where Papa and I saw Mokee. We were in the area where the dinosaur was, so I broke out in sweat and began to shake because I knew he could literally be under our canoe! I told the men to keep their eyes open.

We finally came to a place to tie the canoes. There was a huge field where hundreds of Uganla tribesmen were waiting to take me to the chief. Bachah was the only one who was allowed to go with me, while the others of our tribe had to stay near the river.

The village was only a short walk from the canoes, and as we approached the huts we saw Papa and Tulu tied to poles. I locked eyes with them both as we were taken directly before the chief's hut where he waited, smoking a pipe, flanked by warriors.

As soon as we stood before him, Tulu and Papa were untied and told to immediately go back home. Papa and I tried to hug each other, but one of their tribesmen came between us. The chief then said that I would have to stay and become his daughter that he lost.

Papa and I looked at each other in shock. We were just reunited and now were told we would never see each other again!

"Papa, Papa, don't let them take me!" I cried as one of the tribesmen poked his spear into Papa's side to prod him to leave.

Chaos suddenly erupted. An all-too-familiar roar bellowed from the river. It was Mokee! Yelling and screaming exploded from the frantic tribespeople, and the next thing I knew, we were all running to the river to see the beast, even the old chief.

As we came to the edge of the field, we saw Mokee fully rising up out of the water and approaching the tribesmen on land. He was massive and had a tail as long as a kapok tree. When it moved through the water it made waves that caused the canoes to begin washing down stream. That gave me an idea.

I remembered the left-over rabbit meat from lunch in my knapsack, and recalled how back in the cave the dinosaur ate the rabbit meat we threw at it. I quickly threw what food I had in one of the canoes, hoping that Mokee would get a whiff of it and follow it down stream.

Success!

The massive animal immediately followed the canoe downstream. And because the current was so fast, the canoes quickly sailed ahead of Mokee.

As soon as the dinosaur was out of sight, all of the tribesmen began to pound each other on the back, relieved and happy. Papa and I were embracing each other when the chief walked over. Papa stood in front of me protectively, his face set and fierce.

But instead of reaching for me, the chief extended his hand to Papa.

"Please. Stay. We will have a celebration of peace."

He was not going to keep me for his daughter!

Chapter Thirteen

One God

At the village center, Papa and I were given seats of honor next to the chief, and they stuffed us full of delicious food. In fact, some of the things I ate I had never tasted before. While Papa and the chief smoked a peace pipe together, the chief told Papa that I was truly a beautiful girl, but asked why I stunk so badly.

I raised my eyebrows and looked at Papa embarrassed. He began to laugh and said it was the hakonish that I had all over me to keep the mosquitos away.

The chief chuckled. "Perhaps that was why the beast ran away."

As we laughed together, it occurred to Papa that it was a good opportunity to talk about the one and only true God that our tribe worshipped. Papa started with the story of creation and how the world and everything in it was perfect at first, but how sin messed everything up.

He also explained that death came into the world because of sin, but our God had a Son named Jesus who came to the world and sacrificed himself for us. The chief listened carefully.

He had heard this story before, but now he had many questions about death and life, and about life after death.

Papa smiled from ear to ear and excitedly told the chief that he could have the same forgiveness of sins now and live forever with Jesus when he died.

As I listened to Papa share God's love, I thought of how proud I was of him. He had been through so much the previous few days, yet he saw the opportunity to share Jesus.

As Papa continued to share, the old weathered chief's eyes began to tear up, and he asked Papa how he could have the same forgiveness. Papa then told him that he must not worship other gods because our God was the only true God.

The chief nodded, agreeing, and called everyone in the village to stand before him. He told his people to go get their gods of stone and wood from their tents and bring them to the village fire ring. There was a great bustle around the village as the tribespeople hurried to their homes and gathered the images of their false gods.

As the people of the tribe gathered at the fire, the chief declared that Jehovah was the true God and anyone that wanted to worship him must throw their gods into the fire.

Immediately, everyone threw them into the fire. As the fire became a huge blaze, the chief repeated what Papa said about receiving eternal life through Jesus, and then everyone bowed their whole bodies to the ground, even the witchdoctor! You could feel a peace and freedom in the air as the evil spirits left and the Holy Spirit began to work in each heart.

Then Papa led them in a prayer of salvation. It was the most wonderful thing I had ever seen in my life. The whole village accepted Jesus! Everyone was hugging, and even Papa and the chief hugged and kissed each other and wept.

The chief also gave me a hug and asked for my forgiveness, which I gladly gave. He told me that he never knew what happened to his daughter and missed her greatly and that he hoped that I would visit him often.

The chief was in for a great surprise. No one but Papa knew that during the celebration, Bachah and Tulu went back home to get his daughter, Rowani.

As we prepared to leave for home, the chief gave Papa his own spear as a symbol of peace and thankfulness for sharing the good news of Jesus.

Papa humbly accepted his gift and said, "I, too, have something for you," he said as Bachah and Tulu walked up to him shoulder to shoulder. They were so tall that the chief could not see what was behind them. But when the men parted, there stood Rowani, his grown daughter.

Papa said, "Chief, here is Rowani, your daughter. She is not dead. She is alive!"

The chief and Rowani stood frozen, looking at each other as reality sunk in. Tears began to flow as they slowly approached each other and embraced and cried. As this was happening, you could hear whispering among the tribe as the news spread from person to person. *Beautiful Rowani is home!* Soon the whole village was surrounding us with cheers of gladness.

Papa looked slightly nervous, but the chief locked arms with him and said, "Aaron, it is okay. It is okay. Thank you for what you have done here today. We are at peace now. We are one!"

Cheers and music and dancing around the fire ensued. The celebration continued as we boarded the canoes. I embraced Aunt Rowani.

"I understand why you choose to live with your own people. They are now believers, and you are safe from the threat of being sacrificed to false gods!"

She tucked a strand of hair behind my ear and stroked my cheek as she bent down to look at me. "We will see each other often since the two villages aren't far from each other. We are all at peace, little one. Thank you."

Papa pushed the canoe into the water, and we both waved goodbye to the celebrating village, smiling as joy filled our hearts.

Chapter Fourteen

A Hit On The Head

We moved to the center of the river steering home, and I sighed, relieved and happy. I smiled, thinking about all the events that took place over the past few days. "Papa, you have never told me how our own people first learned of Jesus."

"I didn't? Well, a box fell from the sky and hit me on the head."

"Oh, Papa," I rolled my eyes. "Really. What happened?" I asked, knowing Papa was just kidding.

"I'm serious!" he said. "I was hunting one day when – Wham! – a box hit me on top of the head."

"But where did the box really come from, Papa?" I asked suspiciously.

"I'll tell you." He explained. "There was a missionary from America."

"America! You mean the Christian nation?" I asked.

"Ah, yes, well sort of," he hemmed. "I've heard things have changed and that they may need missionaries from here to go over there now. But anyway, let me finish the story, you interrupting monkey!"

"Ee ee! Oo oo!," I returned like a monkey, laughing. It was so good to have Papa back.

"This particular missionary lived in Kinshasa," he continued. "Every Christmas, Caleb – we called him Caleeb – would load up his small plane with these boxes and fly around till he saw a village that no one had ever contacted. When he saw me, he threw it out of the plane, and 'Bop!' it hit me on the head. I fell to the ground unconscious and when I woke up I saw things on the ground that I'd never seen before: paper, pencils, candy, and the best thing of all – a Bible."

"Wow! Papa that is wonderful!" I exclaimed. "Is that the Bible you use to teach the tribe every Sunday?"

"Yes, Zualoo," he confirmed, "that is the Bible. They translated it into the Mboshi language just for us, but at that time no one in our tribe could read."

Papa looked at me with a smile because he saw that I had a perplexed look on my face.

"Okay, so what happened next?" I asked right on cue.

"The first box was a test to see if we were a friendly tribe. Every day for a week, I came back to the field and waved my hands and each time the pilot threw another box. On the last day, the whole village went out to see what was happening. This time, the pilot landed his small plane in our field and everyone went out to meet him. And this time he had enough boxes for all the children in the village. We could not understand each other's language, but eventually he and other missionaries came to live with us. They taught us how to read that Bible, and that's how we all came to know Jesus."

"So that is why we get shoeboxes full of gifts every Christmas?" I asked.

"Yes. Look, there's the cave," Papa said as we approached. "I'm willing to paddle faster if you are," he challenged.

"Sounds like a good idea!" I agreed wholeheartedly. We both paddled as hard as we could toward home.

"Papa, do you think we'll ever see Mokee again?" I asked.

"Do you want to?" he asked incredulously.

"Ahh, I guess not," I returned.

From that day on, we never did see Mokee again, but we occasionally thought we could hear his roars in the distance.

We finally came to the last bend in the river and began to see our village. It was getting dark and a heavy fog was setting in. I saw Mama standing on the river's edge waiting to greet us. She was jumping up and down and waving and clapping her hands. She was so glad to see us coming back together just as she had seen us both leave days earlier.

We didn't catch any fish on that trip, but we did see a harvest of souls caught for Jesus.

While we ate a delicious supper Mama had made for us, I said, "Papa, I have a confession."

"OK, I'm listening," he said.

"Well, ahh... well, ahh... well, ahh..." I sputtered.

"Okay, well, ahh... what?" Papa said as he licked his fingers.

"Well, ahh, I left the chim chim and hiluki rocks mama made you in the cave when I was going for help. I know they were a special gift. I'm sorry," I said with a sad face.

"No problem," Papa said. "I guess you'll just have to go get them tomorrow."

"Really?"

"Oh no you won't!" Mama said as she began walking toward the fire to throw food scraps in. "I'll just make another pair. You two are not allowed to go back to that cave – ever!"

Papa winked. I grinned and did the same.

THE END

A Lifetime Adventure

Do you know Jesus like Zualoo and her family do? It is evident in this story that even though they had gone through many challenges, they put their faith in God and his son Jesus.

To them, Jesus was real as he proved himself over and over. He will prove himself to you, too.

Would you like to experience the joy of knowing Jesus personally and be assured that you'd live forever with him in heaven one day?

Here are four things God wants you to know:

#1 You must be saved from your sin
Romans 3:23 says all of us are sinners.
Romans 14:12 says we all have to answer to God for our sin and he will judge us.

#2 You cannot save yourself
"Jesus said, 'I am the way and the truth and the life. No one comes to the Father except through me.'" John 14:6

#3 Jesus paid for our sin by dying on a cross
John 3:16 says, "For God so loved the world (you) that he gave his only begotten son, that whosoever believes in him should not perish but have everlasting life."

#4 You can be saved today

Admit to God that you are a sinner.

Believe in the Lord Jesus and you will be saved (Acts 16:31)

Confess with your mouth that Jesus is Lord and believe in your heart that God raised him from the dead and you will be saved (Romans 10:9)

Did you ask Jesus to save you today?
If so, then welcome to the family of God!
You are now officially a child of his forever!

Write today's date down somewhere in your Bible. You'll be glad you did. This is a special date for you. Please share this good news by emailing us at levinsonhome@bellsouth.net